W9-ADN-895

Quiet, Wyatt!

BY **Bill Maynard**

ILLUSTRATED BY **Frank Remkiewicz**

G. P. PUTNAM'S SONS ▪ NEW YORK

For wonderful Wyatt, my grandson,
who said it was okay to use his name
—B. M.

For Maddy
—F. R.

Text copyright © 1999 by William H. Maynard, Jr. Illustrations copyright © 1999 by Frank Remkiewicz
All rights reserved. This book, or parts thereof, may not be reproduced in any form without permission
in writing from the publisher. G. P. Putnam's Sons, a division of Penguin Putnam Books for Young Readers,
345 Hudson Street, New York, NY 10014. G. P. Putnam's Sons, Reg. U.S. Pat. & Tm. Off.
Published simultaneously in Canada. Printed in Hong Kong by South China Printing Co. (1988) Ltd.
Design by Donna Mark. Text set in Ida.

The illustrations for QUIET, WYATT! are rendered in gouache and colored pencil on colored paper.

Library of Congress Cataloging-in-Publication Data
Maynard, Bill. Quiet, Wyatt! / by Bill Maynard; illustrated by Frank Remkiewicz. p. cm.
Summary: Everyone is always telling Wyatt to be quiet because he's too young, but when he gets mad and
stops talking, it seems that maybe he wasn't so annoying after all. [1. Growth—Fiction. 2. Noise—Fiction.]
I. Remkiewicz, Frank, ill. II. Title. PZ7.M4695Qu 1999 [E]—dc21 97-28183 CIP AC
ISBN 0-399-23217-6   10 9 8 7 6 5 4 3 2 1   FIRST IMPRESSION

The big kids on Wyatt's street were
building a model plane.

Wyatt said, "I'd like to fly it."

But the big kids said, "Quiet, Wyatt.
You're not old enough to fly a plane."

Wyatt's sister was washing the car.
Wyatt said, "I'd like to dry it."
But his sister frowned and said,
"Quiet, Wyatt. You're not big enough
to dry a car."

Wyatt's father took an egg out of
the refrigerator. Wyatt touched it. It
was smooth and cold.

Wyatt said, "I'd like to fry it."

But his father smiled and said,
"Quiet, Wyatt. You're not old enough
to fry an egg."

On Saturday, when Wyatt's family took a walk downtown, Wyatt saw a puppy in the pet store window. The puppy looked soft and fluffy and had big brown eyes.

Wyatt said, "I'd like to buy it."

His mother shook her head. "Quiet, Wyatt. You're not old enough to have a puppy yet."

First Wyatt was sad. Then Wyatt was angry. *Nobody will listen to me,* he thought. *Nobody thinks that I'm big enough or old enough to do anything. But I'll change their minds.*

The next morning, Wyatt got up very early. He put on his father's coat and hat. He picked up his father's briefcase and went outside.

"**I'm Wyatt!**" he shouted. "Someday I'll be the biggest kid on the street."

His neighbors opened their windows. "Quiet, Wyatt," they called. "We're trying to sleep."

That afternoon, when all the big kids went to a football game, Wyatt followed them. During a time-out in the game, Wyatt ran onto the field.

"I'm Wyatt!" he shouted. "And someday I'm going to be big enough to kick a football all the way up to the sky."

The people watching the game began to yell. "QUIET, WYATT!" they shouted. "YOU'RE INTERRUPTING THE GAME!"

Poor Wyatt. He ran to the river
at the edge of town.

"**I'm Wyatt!**" he shouted. "And
someday I'm going to be big enough
to catch the biggest fish in this river."

"River...river...river," repeated
an echo.

The fishermen didn't want Wyatt
to scare the fish. "Quiet, Wyatt," they
called. And the echo said:

"Quiet...quiet...quiet.
Wyatt...Wyatt...Wyatt."

"Even the echo doesn't want to
listen to me," said Wyatt. "*Nobody*
wants to listen to me. So why should
I say anything at all?" And from then
on, Wyatt was quiet.

The big kids lost their airplane. Wyatt knew where it was.

But Wyatt was quiet.

Wyatt's sister polished the family car until it was all dry
and shiny. Wyatt saw a big black rain cloud approaching.
But Wyatt was quiet.

Wyatt's father left an egg on the kitchen counter.
Wyatt saw it start to roll toward the edge. But Wyatt
was quiet.

Splat!

The mailman drove up. When he got out of his truck, he was
carrying all the mail for Wyatt's whole street. Wyatt saw that
the mailman's shoelaces were untied. But Wyatt was quiet.
Crash!

Then Wyatt saw something coming up his street. It was the soft, fluffy puppy with the big brown eyes. It ran right past Wyatt and hid underneath the mailman's truck.

The pet store owner ran up and down the street. "Have you seen a puppy?" he asked. But Wyatt was quiet.

The police chief ran up the street. "Have you seen a puppy?" he asked. But Wyatt was quiet.

By now all the people on Wyatt's street had come out of their houses.

Oh, no! The mailman was getting into his truck. Wyatt *wanted* to be quiet, but he was so afraid that the puppy might get hurt by the truck that he just *couldn't* keep quiet any longer.

"THE PUPPY IS HIDING UNDER THE MAILMAN'S TRUCK!" Wyatt shouted.

Quickly, the mailman got out of his truck. Wyatt crawled under the truck and saved the puppy. Then the pet store owner took the puppy back to the pet store, and Wyatt waved good-bye.

"It's a good thing that Wyatt said something," one of the neighbors remarked. And all the people on Wyatt's street agreed.

The next day, people began to treat Wyatt differently.

"Fly it, Wyatt."

"Dry it, Wyatt."

"Fry it, Wyatt."

On Saturday, when Wyatt and his family took a walk downtown, Wyatt couldn't wait to see the puppy in the pet store window. And the puppy jumped up and down because he was so glad to see Wyatt.

Wyatt's parents remembered how Wyatt had spoken up to save the puppy, and they were very proud of him. They pointed to the puppy and said, "Let's buy it, Wyatt!"

Now Wyatt was really happy. He had his own soft, fluffy puppy with big brown eyes. And nobody ever said "Quiet, Wyatt" anymore.

Well, *hardly* ever.